PRAIRIE
Born

PRAIRIE *Born*

poem by DAVE BOUCHARD

paintings by PETER SHOSTAK

ORCA BOOK PUBLISHERS

I hope they leave some food for me

Orca Book Publishers gratefully acknowledges the support for our publishing
programs provided by the following agencies: the Department of Canadian
Heritage, the Canada Council for the Arts, and the British Columbia
Ministry of Small Business, Tourism and Culture.

Orca Book Publishers
PO Box 5626, Station B
Victoria, BC V8R 6S4
Canada

Orca Book Publishers
PO Box 468
Custer, WA 98240-0468
USA

Canadian Cataloguing in Publication Data
Bouchard, Dave, 1952 –
Prairie born

ISBN 1-55143-092-4
1. Prairie Provinces—Juvenile poetry. 2. Prairie Provinces in art.
I. Shostak, Peter, 1943– II. Title.
PS8553.O759P72 1997   jC811'.54 C97–910428–9
PZ7.B6589Pr 1997

Library of Congress Catalog Card Number: 97-67365

Design by Christine Toller
Printed and bound in Hong Kong

99 98 97   5 4 3 2 1

For Mom and Dad on the occasion of their Golden Anniversary.
D.B.

For my first fan, the one who encouraged my early creative efforts
and gave me the time and space to grow as an artist.
For my mom.
P.S.

At night, when I closed my eyes to go to sleep, I could still see all those rocks

And the prairie continues to live in my heart
It's much more than memories that tell me apart
It's the wind and the sun, the cold and the snow
Only things that a child of the prairie will know.

If I had a penny for each time I spoke
Of cold howling winds, of deep drifting snow
Of darkness of winter on route to the rink
Of so many memories, I smile as I think
Knowing full well that others who've never lived there
Will nod and listen but don't really care
As *"Mornin', fine day"* means nothing much more
To me it means …

Next year we will make a bigger rink

To me it means: "Come in and please shut the door.
  Will the kids be all right? Should I plug in the car?
  If I start shovelling now will I get very far?
  Will I have to start over before I am done?
  Will the wind blow it back? It must weigh a ton!
  Fill your cup up, let's visit … Remember the time
  When the snow bank was up past the telephone line?
  Here's me in a picture, I'm shovelling the drive.
  The snow line is over the roof on three sides.
  Say what? You can top that — well try this for size,
  I'd shovelled three hours and to my surprise,
  That night as I came home, d'you know what I saw?
  The wind blew it … "

We can take turns using the toboggan

I know that I'm rambling but all this is true
It's more than a memory of times that I knew
It answers the mystery of what lies in our souls
Where nature's the teacher for young and for old.

It shapes us from childhood through sun and through rain
Compels us to live for life's pleasures and pain
And the secret of me from the day of my birth
Is the nurturing seasons and rich prairie earth.

How many sacks of potatoes will we have?

You've come to know spring as when snow finally leaves
And thoughts turn to songbirds and flowers that please
But the truth of this time of the year's not in buds,
It's rubbers and boots, filthy doormats and mud.

And yet we found dry spots on which we could play
With marbles or jump ropes, on hard, packed down clay.
We all knew a puddle was somehow to find
Our brand new white baseball, but we didn't mind.

For boys, boots are never high enough

And we took out our bikes just as soon as we could,
As mom packed our parkas, our toques and our hoods
And our vitamins, porridge and cod liver oil
Like kids on the farm we would thrive near fresh soil.

And the prairie continues to live in my heart
It's much more than memories that tell me apart
It's the wind and the sun, the cold and the snow
Only things that a child of the prairie will know.

See, we made it

A child dreams of summer as picnics and games,
And we from the prairie have thoughts much the same
The difference for me is in how I now look
The answer you'll read on my face like a book.

I'm young yet I'm wrinkled and know why it's so
It's from years of playing baseball, from crouching down low
My eyes always squinting in dust and bright sun
These lines in my face are from years of good fun.

How many kids still play scrub?

When we think of summer there's always a bug,
A mosquito that hovers in swarms thick as rugs
While playing or eating or just walking outside
We'd fight them and lose, we'd run and we'd hide.

Yet the prairie continues to live in my heart
It's much more than memories that tell me apart
It's the wind and the sun, the cold and the snow
Only things that a child of the prairie will know.

It's too far away

Go back for a moment, remember *your* fall
Leaves changing colours, you raked and you hauled
I too know this season, but for me it's much more
And the earth knows my secret's not found on her floor.

It's a gift from the mountains that started at sea.
It's fresh, crisp new air and it's not only me,
Any child of the prairie will tell you for them
That the air of September means winter again.

It's going to be a long day

And I'll always remember the times that I stood
Alone on the prairie, 'neath the stars when I could
My gaze towards heaven, my feet on the clay
While standing there breathing, I learned how to pray.

And the prairie continues to live in my heart
It's much more than memories that tell me apart
It's the wind and the sun, the cold and the snow
Only things that a child of the prairie will know.

This will probably be my best angel

You've all heard the stories of snow and of cold
As Service and Kurelek with passion have told
Of times in their lives when records were set
Well, *I've* lived through winter and I'll not forget.

That the cold on its own is a thing to be feared
But coupled with harsh wind as darkness draws near
It teaches respect for what nature can be
And it's taken the credit for what's come to be me.

Maybe I will get new skates for my birthday

You see …

My hair's mostly wind, my eyes filled with grit
My skin's white then brown, my lips chapped and split
I've lain on the prairie and heard grasses sigh
I've stared at the vast open bowl of the sky
I've seen all the castles and faces in clouds
My home is the prairie and for that I am proud …

Wood was our sole source of fuel

And that prairie continues to live in our hearts
It's much more than memories that tell us apart
It's the wind! It's the sun! It's the cold! It's the snow!
Only things that we kids from the prairie will know.

It's your turn to come over on Sunday